ILLUMINATION

Arts

PUBLISHING COMPANY, INC.

P.O. Box 1865, Bellevue, WA 98009

Tel: 425-644-7185 ✽ 888-210-8216 (orders only) ✽ Fax: 425-644-9274

liteinfo@illumin.com ✽ www.illumin.com

Library of Congress Cataloging-in-Publication Data

McKinley, Cindy, 1968-
    One smile / written by Cindy McKinley ; illustrated by Mary Gregg Byrne.
      p. cm.
    Summary: When a child smiles at a stranger, she sets off a chain of kindness that eventually comes full circle.
    ISBN 0-935699-23-6
    [1. Smile—Fiction. 2. Kindness—Fiction.] I. Byrne, Mary Gregg, 1951-, ill. II. Title.

PZ7.M19867 On 2002
[E]—dc21

                 2002024506

Third printing 2005
Published in the United States of America
Printed in Singapore by Star Standard Industries
Book Designer: Molly Murrah, Murrah & Company, Kirkland, WA

ILLUMINATION ARTS PUBLISHING COMPANY, INC.
is a member of Publishers in Partnership - replanting our nation's forests.

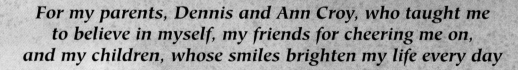

*For my parents, Dennis and Ann Croy, who taught me
to believe in myself, my friends for cheering me on,
and my children, whose smiles brighten my life every day*

Cindy McKinley

*For all my friends and family who patiently posed for me
and my dear friends at G.A.S.P. (the Great Art Support grouP)*

Mary Gregg Byrne

CONTENTS
PUBLISHING COMPANY, INC.
BELLEVUE, WASHINGTON

OneSmile

Written by Cindy McKinley
Illustrated by Mary Gregg Byrne

One breezy summer morning, Katie was walking through the park with her mother. "Hurry up sweetheart," her mother urged, "or we'll be late for the bus."

"Oh Mommy," said the little girl, "I sure hope our van is fixed in time for Grandpa's birthday party."

Just then they noticed a sad young man sitting alone on a bench. Katie stopped for a moment and smiled brightly at him.

The young man had lost his job and was feeling very discouraged. Dozens of people had walked by that morning, but no one seemed to notice him. Then this little girl appeared and touched his heart with the sweetest smile he'd ever seen. He suddenly felt inspired to start looking for a new job.

As he hurried down the busy street, the man saw a woman struggling to change a tire. "Let me help you with that," he offered without hesitation.

The woman had been driving to an important meeting when she heard a loud *thump thump thump* and pulled over to the side of the road. Many people had passed by before this helpful young man came to her rescue.

Later, as she finished lunch, the woman was still feeling grateful for the young man's help, so she left an extra large tip.

"Thanks! Thanks a lot!" the waitress called out.

On her way home, the waitress decided to surprise her children. Using
the extra tip money, she picked up sodas, potato salad, and fried chicken.
Then she bought the soccer ball her children had been hoping for.

"Surprise!" she called out. "Let's go have a picnic!"

"Wow, Mom!" her youngest boy exclaimed. "You're the best! Can we invite the girl next door? She's new in town and doesn't have any friends yet."

"Good idea," his mother said. "Let's invite the whole family."

The little girl had been sitting alone in her room missing her grandparents and friends when the phone rang. She couldn't believe the boy next door was calling. *Maybe we could be friends,* she thought.

The girl and her parents brought some homemade brownies, and they all enjoyed a very special evening together in the park.

After she got ready for bed, the little girl couldn't wait to call her grandma back home on the farm. "Guess what, Nana! We had a really fun picnic with our neighbors! I think I'm going to like it here after all."

Nana could hear the excitement in her granddaughter's voice. "Well honey, I sure miss having you around," she said, "but I'm glad to know you're making new friends."

After hanging up, Nana took out her favorite stationery. Wanting to share the good feeling, she wrote a letter to each of her grandchildren. Inside every envelope she tucked a special sheet of animal stickers.

Nana's youngest grandson was about to leave for the doctor's office when his letter arrived. All morning, he had been nervous about getting a shot. But after seeing the animal stickers, he forgot all about being afraid.

In the doctor's waiting room, the boy sat next to a sad little girl with a cast on her arm. "Here," he said, "maybe my new animal stickers will help you feel better."

The girl stopped crying and carefully placed the stickers on her cast. As the children giggled together, her father sighed with relief. His daughter had been upset for hours, and now she was happy again. After taking her home, the father rushed back to his busy auto shop.

That night a young man walked into the shop. "Do you have any job openings?" he asked. "I work hard and I'm good at fixing cars."

Still remembering the little boy's kindness in the doctor's office, the girl's father decided to give this stranger a chance. "Well," he said, "I could use some extra help. Let's give it a try."

The grateful young man arrived early for work the next morning. His first job was completing the repairs on a dark green van. Just before noon, he returned the keys to a woman and her daughter.

"I'm glad I could help fix your van," he said.

"Thank you!" said the little girl. "Now we can go to my grandpa's birthday party after all!" She smiled brightly at the man. It was a smile he remembered very well...

...a smile that was changing the world.

Thoughtful Questions to Ponder With Your Family:

1. What qualities make a person kind?
2. Who has been kind to you? What kind things has someone done for you?
3. In what ways have you been kind to others?
4. Do you know someone who could use an act of kindness? Who is it? What could you do?
5. What kind things could you do for:

… your parents?   … your brother or sister?
… your teacher?   … your neighbors?
… your bus driver?   … your mailman?
… your doctor or dentist?   … a far-away relative?
… an elderly friend?   … the Earth?

Here's a Challenge!

Can your family work together to think of 20 simple acts of kindness? Write them down and discuss them together. As someone in your family does each kind act, draw a "☺" next to it! Then log on to www.cindymckinley.com and share your family's ideas!

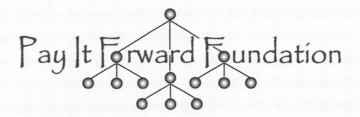

Imagine what would happen if Katie's simple kindness just kept growing. Trevor, the fictional 12-year-old hero of the novel *Pay It Forward*, thinks of quite an idea. He describes it this way: "You see, I do something real good for three people. And then when they ask how they can pay it back, I say they have to Pay It Forward. To three more people. Each. So nine people get helped. Then those people have to do twenty-seven. Then it sort of spreads out, see. To eighty-one. Then two hundred forty-three. Then seven hundred twenty-nine. Then two thousand, one hundred eighty-seven. See how big it gets?"

Working with Trevor's plan, the **Pay It Forward Foundation** has been established to educate and inspire young students to realize that they can change the world. By bringing the author's vision and related educational materials into classrooms across the country, students and their teachers will be encouraged to formulate their own ideas of how they can "Pay It Forward."

"You don't need much to change the entire world for the better. You can start with the most ordinary ingredients. You can start with the world you've got."

The Pay It Forward Foundation
P.O. Box 552
Cambria, CA 93428
www.payitforwardfoundation.org / www.payitforwardmovement.org

	DATE DUE		